Dedicated to my wife, Amy, and two boys, for the happiness you give me every day.
I love you and wish you happiness, forever and ever. –Michael

Follow us for news of new books and giveaways at PiccoPuppy.com and
@PiccoPuppy on Facebook and Instagram #iwishyouhappinessbook #piccopuppy

Also by Michael Wong

Bedtime for Picco Puppy   *Picco Puppy's Counting Book*
Picco Puppy Loves Soccer   *Picco Puppy Says Yes*
Picco Puppy Loves Football   *Picco Puppy Says Thank You*

Thank you to the Kickstarter and Indiegogo community, family and friends,
Jay Miletsky, and Miriam Pinedo for your generous support.

Special thanks to Ann Baratashvili, for your beautiful illustrations; and
David Miles, for your beautiful cover design and invaluable guidance.

Font Credits

Lost Brush by Stripes Studio   Century Schoolbook by Morris Fuller Benton
Marck Script by Denis Masharov   Copse by Dan Rhatigan
Cormorant Upright by Christian Thalmann   Josefin Sans by Santiago Orozco

First published in 2020 by Picco Puppy
Marketing Munch Pty Ltd DBA Picco Puppy, PO Box 103 Killara NSW 2071 Australia
Picco Puppy is a registered trademark of Marketing Munch Pty Ltd

ISBN 978-1-76133-182-4

I Wish You Happiness

MICHAEL WONG • ANN BARATASHVILI

Emmett, I wish you
dreams and *aspirations*,
to spread your wings and
reach for the stars.

I wish you *courage* and *strength*, *Emmett*, for the magic begins at the end of your comfort zone.

I wish you *imagination* and *creativity*, for the world is a blank canvas to paint your masterpiece.

Emmett, I wish you *adventure* and *curiosity*,
to go where there is no path
and leave a trail.

I wish you *health* and *well-being*, for they are worth more than all the riches in the world.

I wish you *peace* and *tranquility*, to listen
to the birds and gaze at the stars, *Emmett.*

I wish you *knowledge* and *wisdom*, for they are the foundations of a successful life.

I wish you *grit* and *resilience*, to never ever give up.

Emmett, I wish you success and *prosperity*, to trust yourself and your ability to succeed.

I wish you *luck* and *opportunity*, for the more you try, the luckier you get.

I wish you *faith* and *hope*, to believe everything will be all right.

Emmett, I wish you family and friendships, for they are life's greatest sources of happiness.

I wish you *joy* and *laughter*, Emmett, to laugh long and loud until you gasp for breath.

I wish you *kindness* and *generosity*, for no act of kindness is ever wasted, no matter how small.

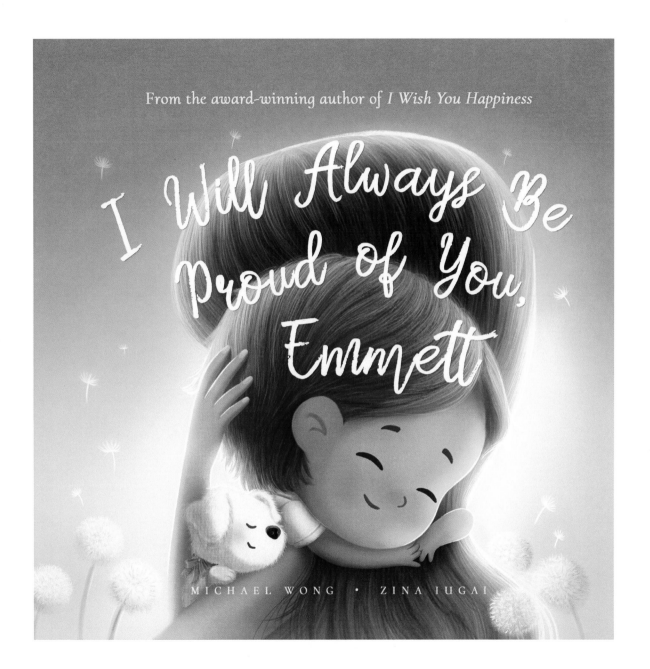

From the award-winning author of *I Wish You Happiness*

I Will Always Be Proud of You, Emmett

MICHAEL WONG • ZINA IUGAI

Also by Michael Wong, *I Will Always Be Proud of You, Emmett*.
Available on Amazon and PiccoPuppy.com.

Made in United States
North Haven, CT
29 September 2022

24680132R00022

Can You Spot the Dogs?

There are seventeen dogs and one cat in the book. Emmett, can you spot them all?

Beagle	Cavalier King Charles Spaniel	Dalmatian	French Bulldog	German Shepherd	Golden Retriever
Jack Russell Terrier	Labrador Retriever	Maltese	Pomeranian	Poodle	Pug
Saint Bernard	Shiba Inu	Siamese Cat	Welsh Corgi	West Highland Terrier	Yorkshire Terrier

Can You Spot Your Name?
Your name appears nine times in the story. Can you spot them all?

We hope you enjoyed the book.
Your opinion matters. Please leave a review on Amazon and PiccoPuppy.com.
Tell others why you enjoyed this book. Thank you.

Hardcover · Personalized · Bilingual

I Wish You Happiness is available as a 10x10 inch jacketed hardcover, and personalized, bilingual, French, German, Italian, and Spanish editions.

A thoughtful gift for baby showers, birthdays, and graduations. Available on Amazon, PiccoPuppy.com, and in bookstores.

Michael Wong is an award-winning children's author. He is passionate about creating empowering, diverse, and inclusive books for children. Michael lives with his wife and two children in Sydney, Australia.

Ann Baratashvili is an illustrator and concept artist. She won first prize in the 2009 DeviantArt/Wacom "Bring Your Vision to Life: Dreams" contest. Ann lives with her husband and son in Tbilisi, Georgia.

Can You Spot the Famous People?

Emmett, no matter what obstacles you face, believe in yourself and all that you are—just like these famous people did. Can you spot all five in the book?

Can you spot a young Neil Armstrong?

Neil is a famous astronaut who became the first person to walk on the moon in 1969. Before that, he was an experimental research test pilot, which is a very dangerous job.

Can you spot a young Katherine Johnson?

Katherine is a mathematician whose calculations helped send the Apollo 11 rocket carrying Neil Armstrong and his fellow astronauts to the moon.

Can you spot a young Amelia Earhart?

Amelia was the first female aviator to fly solo across the Atlantic Ocean. She helped to create The Ninety-Nines, an international organization of women pilots.

Can you spot a young J. K. Rowling?

Twelve publishers rejected Joanne's first book. She had to wait a year before her book was finally published. Her Harry Potter books went on to become the best-selling book series in history.

Can you spot a young Alexander Selkirk?

Alexander famously spent four years as a castaway on an uninhabited island. His survival story inspired Daniel Defoe's Robinson Crusoe, often credited as the first English novel, published in 1719.

Emmett, I wish you all those wonderful things, but most of all . . .

I wish you happiness!

I wish you *love* and *affection*, *Emmett*, to fill your beautiful heart with an ocean of joy.